Nanny Fox

Georgie Adams + Selina Young

Orion
Children's Books

Arnold Fox loved chickens.

Not to eat – just as friends.

He spent hours watching them picking at this, pecking at that
and laying their eggs all over the place.

The Buff Orpingtons were the noisiest of hens.

Mrs Buff Orpington fluffed out her feathers to make
herself more important than all the rest.

Arnold loved to see the chicks hatch.

He would hide near a clutch of eggs, listen to the soft tap, tap, tap inside, then watch as one by one . . . crack! Each egg split and out clambered a tiny yellow chick, wet and wobbly.

Eating them was unthinkable.

Arnold's family thought differently.

"Chickens are for eating," said Ma Fox, plonking down a fat hen for supper one night.

"It's traditional," said Pa Fox, tucking into a tasty leg.

"And scrummy!" said Arnold's sister, Lucy.

"I'll stick to peanut butter sandwiches, thank you," said Arnold.

"Eating chickens is what foxes do best," Pa Fox said.

"And catching them is fun!" said Ma Fox.

For weeks Ma Fox had been teaching her children to steal chickens from the farm.

She showed them how to creep through the woods at night . . .
Sneak up to the henhouse . . .
Wriggle through a hole . . .
and **snatch** a sleepy hen or two.

Then, they would dash off with their squawking bundles, before the farmer could get out of bed and chase them away.

Poor Arnold was horrified.

Perhaps, he thought sadly, it's time for me to leave home.

One day, as Arnold was passing the henhouse, he saw a notice.

He knocked at the door.
Mrs Buff Orpington opened it – and fainted.

"I've come about the job," said Arnold when she had recovered.

"I'd love to look after your chicks."

"Foxes don't look after chickens," said Mrs. Buff Orpington.
"They eat them."

Arnold thought of his family.
"Some do," he said. "But I don't."

Just then the chicks appeared. They liked the look of Arnold.
He was soft and furry and had gentle eyes. They were too
young to know about foxes.

Mrs Buff Orpington was a very busy bird and needed help quickly.

"When can you start?" she asked.

"Today," said Arnold.

"Good," said Mrs Buff Orpington. "You'll do.
"But remember, I've got six chicks. I've counted them twice.
"If one should disappear.." she said, looking hard at Arnold,
"I'll send for the farmer at once."

Arnold went home to pack his bag and say goodbye.

"Where are you going?" asked Ma Fox.

"To the farm," said Arnold.

"What for?" said Pa Fox. "It's not suppertime."

"I've got a job," said Arnold.

"Doing what?" asked Lucy and Dennis.

"Looking after... things," said Arnold vaguely.
He couldn't explain about the chicks. His family
would never understand.

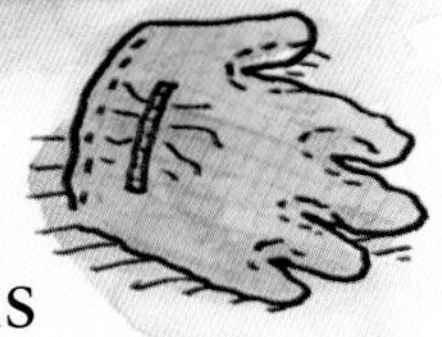

So Arnold left home and became Nanny Fox,
and the chicks loved him dearly. Keeping all six chicks
together wasn't easy. They wandered off in all directions at once.
Arnold spent the first day counting them, again and again.

One,
two,
three,
four,
five...
Six.

Next day, Arnold found an
old bicycle. It had a basket on
the front, just big enough to hold six chicks.

So they spent the day riding
round the farmyard meeting the geese and the goats,
the pigs and the cows.

Arnold taught the chicks all kinds of things.
He taught them how to ride on his back, run egg and spoon
races across the field, and stuff pillows with feathers for
a battle at bedtime.

The chicks loved this game. Mrs Buff Orpington did not.
There were feathers all over the henhouse.

That night, as the hens huddled fast asleep, two young foxes came creeping through the shadows. They padded silently round the henhouse and wriggled through a hole.

It was Lucy and Dennis, hunting on their own for the first time.

Then came the most terrible screeching as Dennis snatched Mrs Buff Orpington from her perch and Lucy pulled her into the yard.

Arnold ran to see what was the matter.

"She's mine!" cried Lucy, tugging Mrs Buff Orpington to the right.

"I got her first!" shouted Dennis, pulling her to the left.

Mrs Buff Orpington squawked at the top of her voice.

"Stop it!" ordered Arnold. "Put her down!"

By this time, all the other animals had woken up.
The geese were honking, the goats were bleating, the pigs
were snorting and the cows were mooing.

Suddenly, lights went on in the farmhouse.
There was an angry yell from the farmer.

Dennis and Lucy ran home and told Ma Fox and Pa Fox
what had happened.

"Arnold was guarding the henhouse," said Dennis.
"He pulled my ear," said Lucy.
"Hm," said Ma Fox thoughtfully. "Now Arnold is at the farm, we shall have to hunt somewhere else."
There was no fat hen for supper that night.

Back at the farm, Mrs Buff Orpington lay in a crumpled heap.
Arnold lifted her gently on to a pile of straw.
He smoothed her ruffled feathers.

The frightened chicks clambered out of the henhouse. Mrs Buff Orpington opened a beady eye and saw Arnold bending over her.

"Did you just try to eat me?" she croaked.

Arnold shook his head.

"Nanny Fox tried to save you!"
chirped the chicks
as they clung to Arnold's fur.

Mrs Buff Orpington sighed with relief.
"Nanny Fox loves chickens," said Arnold.
"Not to eat – just as friends!"